Mater joins his best bud Lightning McQueen for a race through
Japan, Italy and London. To find out what happens when Mater is
mistaken for a secret agent, read along with me in your book.
You will know it's time to turn the page when you hear this sound...
Let's begin now. Start your engines, it's go time!

Narrator	David Jeremiah
Francesco Bernoulli	John Turturro
Lightning McQueen	Owen Wilson
Mater	Larry the Cable Guy
Grem	Joe Mantegna
Acer	Peter Jacobson
Holley Shiftwell	Emily Mortimer
Finn McMissile	Michael Caine
Professor Z	Thomas Kretschmann
Sir Miles Axlerod	Eddie Izzard
The Lord Steward	Sean Barrett

Walt Disney RECORDS

℗ 2012 Walt Disney Records © Disney Enterprises, Inc.
Unauthorized duplication and use prohibited.

First published by Parragon in 2012
Parragon
Queen Street House
4 Queen Street
Bath BA1 1HE, UK

Bath · New York · Singapore · Hong Kong · Cologne · Delhi
Melbourne · Amsterdam · Johannesburg · Shenzhen

Lightning McQueen had just returned to Radiator Springs. He was celebrating his fourth Piston Cup win at the Wheel Well restaurant with Sally. But Mater wanted to spend time with Lightning, so the tow truck pretended to be a waiter at the restaurant. And that's when the trouble started....

On TV, Sir Miles Axlerod was talking about the World Grand Prix. All the fastest cars in the world were going to compete – all except Lightning McQueen. The race car wanted to take some time off.

An Italian race car named Francesco Bernoulli was convinced he would win. "Lightning McQueen would not have a chance against Francesco!"

Before Lightning realized what was happening, he and Mater had called into the show and then Lightning had agreed to enter the race!

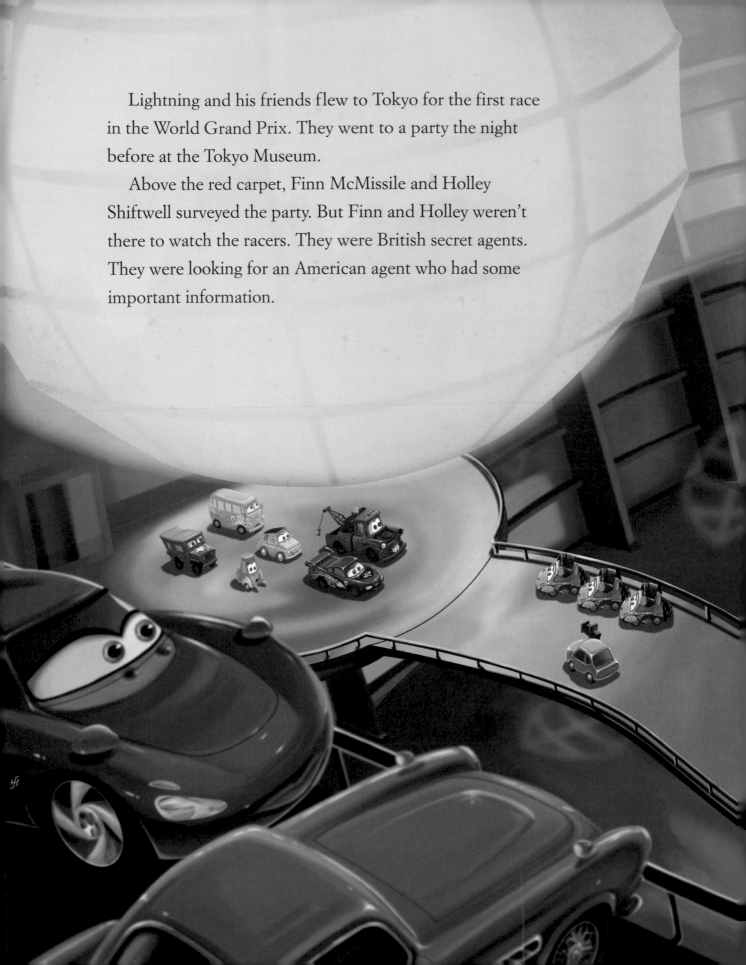

Lightning and his friends flew to Tokyo for the first race in the World Grand Prix. They went to a party the night before at the Tokyo Museum.

Above the red carpet, Finn McMissile and Holley Shiftwell surveyed the party. But Finn and Holley weren't there to watch the racers. They were British secret agents. They were looking for an American agent who had some important information.

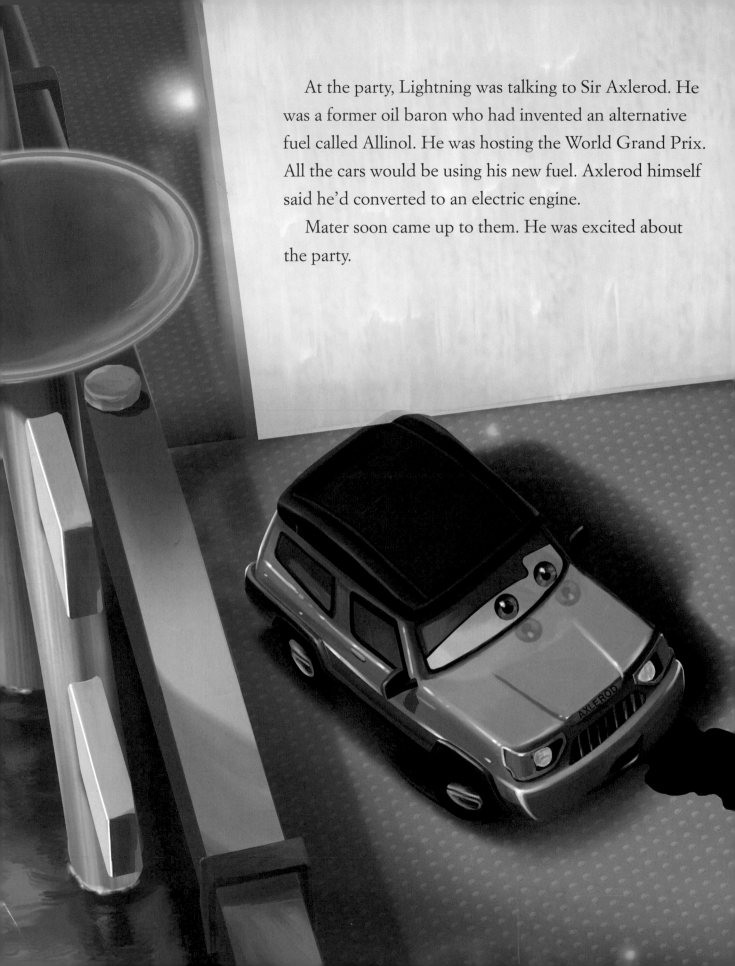

At the party, Lightning was talking to Sir Axlerod. He was a former oil baron who had invented an alternative fuel called Allinol. He was hosting the World Grand Prix. All the cars would be using his new fuel. Axlerod himself said he'd converted to an electric engine.

Mater soon came up to them. He was excited about the party.

When Lightning spotted a pool of oil under Mater, he got upset. "Mater, you have to get a hold of yourself! You're making a scene."

Mater was embarrassed. "But I never leak oil. Never." He hurried off to the bathroom.

As he left the bathroom stall, Mater interrupted a fight. One of the cars in the fight was the American agent.

When Mater wasn't paying attention, the secret agent saw his chance. He planted the top-secret information on the tow truck. A second later, Grem and Acer, the other two cars, chased Mater away. "Get outta here!"

Out in the hallway, Holley stopped Mater. She spoke to him in a quiet voice. "When can I see you again?"

Mater was surprised. "Well, let's see, tomorrow I'll be out there at the races." He thought Holley wanted to go on a date.

But Holley didn't want a date. She had realized Mater was carrying secret information. She thought *he* was the American agent!

The next day was the first race of the World Grand Prix. Mater and the rest of the Radiator Springs crew were busy in the pit. They had to make sure Lightning McQueen was in tip-top shape to compete.

Before long, the starting lights clicked from red to yellow to green and the race began.

But soon disaster struck! One of the racers started to smoke. His engine was blown. A moment later, another race car blew an engine and skidded out of control.

Just then, a voice came through Mater's headset. "Get out of the pit now."

Mater recognized that voice. "Hey, I know you! You're that girl from the party last night. You want to do our date right now?"

Mater left the arena to meet the pretty car.

Mater looked for Holley outside the racetrack. She spoke to him over the headset when she saw him try to buy flowers. "No! Don't go in anywhere. Just keep moving."

Mater replied, forgetting that Lightning could hear him. "Stay outside. Got you."

Lightning was confused, but he moved to the outside of the track.

Meanwhile, Mater spotted Finn McMissile fighting off some tough cars.

Mater didn't know Finn was a secret agent. He thought he was watching a karate demonstration. He cheered excitedly.

Lightning told Mater to turn off the headset. Moving outside had cost him the lead. He tried to catch up, but another car won the race.

Afterward, Lightning was furious with Mater. "Why were you yelling things at me while I was racing? I lost the race because of you!"

Mater was shocked. "I'm sorry. I didn't mean to—"

But Lightning was too mad to listen. "This is exactly why I don't bring you along to these things."

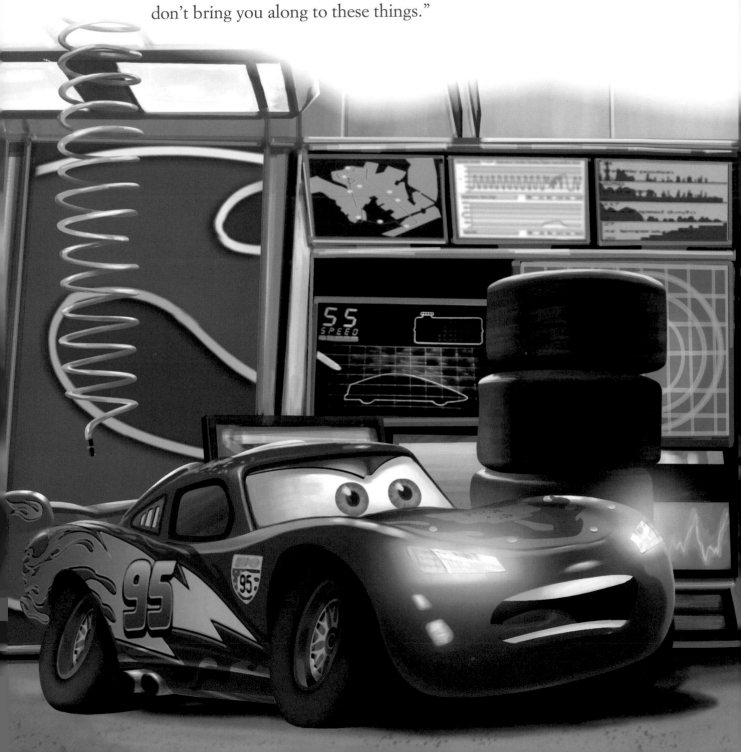

Mater offered to do something. "Maybe if I, oh I don't know, talked to somebody and explained what happened, I could help?"

Lightning shook his head. "I don't need your help. I don't *want* your help...."

Mater felt terrible. He didn't want Lightning to lose any more races because of him. Mater decided it would be better if he left.

The next morning, Mater went to the airport to fly home to
Radiator Springs. But he never made it onto the plane. Finn showed
up, disguised as a security guard. "Come with me please, sir."

Before long, Mater found himself on a private jet. Holley was
there. She and Finn showed Mater a picture of an engine. Then
they asked for his help for a top-secret mission. They needed to find
out what was causing so many of the race cars' engines to explode.
Mater would need to go undercover with a disguise.

Mater agreed. "Well, okay." Still one thing bothered him. "But
you know I'm just a tow truck, right?"

Holley and Finn didn't believe him. They still thought Mater was
a secret agent – and a very good one!

Once they landed in Porto Corsa, Italy, the plan began to unfold. Disguised as a Russian tow truck, Mater snuck into a meeting of bad cars. There he learned about a sinister plot to hurt the racers in the World Grand Prix.

A boxy, German car wearing a monocle addressed the bad cars. His name was Professor Z. He wanted to become powerful. So he came up with a plan to use radiation guns disguised as TV cameras. The radiation would heat up the Allinol fuel inside the cars, causing the racers' engines to explode.

Meanwhile, the second race of the World Grand Prix was about to start nearby.

This was Francesco's home turf. He addressed the crowd. "*Bellissima!* Thank you for your support." He was sure he would beat Lightning.

The race began and the cars zipped around the course. Before long, a few cars' engines blew up. That caused one crash after another. It was a pile-up nightmare! The bad guys had struck again.

Everyone suspected something was wrong with the Allinol.

After the last hairpin turn, Lightning nosed out Francesco for the win.

Francesco couldn't believe it. "*Bah!* This is impossible!"

Lightning was thrilled. "That's what I'm talkin' about. *Ka-chow!*"

The other racers decided not to use Allinol at the next race, but Lightning told the press he would.

At the meeting, Mater realized his friend Lightning would be the next target. He started to shake and moved toward the door. Then he received an urgent message from Holley. "Abort the mission. Get out of there. Get out of there right now."

As Mater tried to escape, his cover was blown.
Professor Z spotted him. "It's the American spy!"

At first Mater froze. "Dad gum." Then he made a quick
getaway using the parachute gadget Holley had given him.

Mater hurried to the racetrack to find Lightning. He pushed his way through the crowd, trying to get his friend's attention. "Let me through! Let me through!"

But Lightning didn't see him. Before Mater could reach his friend, Professor Z and the bad cars captured him. They knocked the tow truck out.

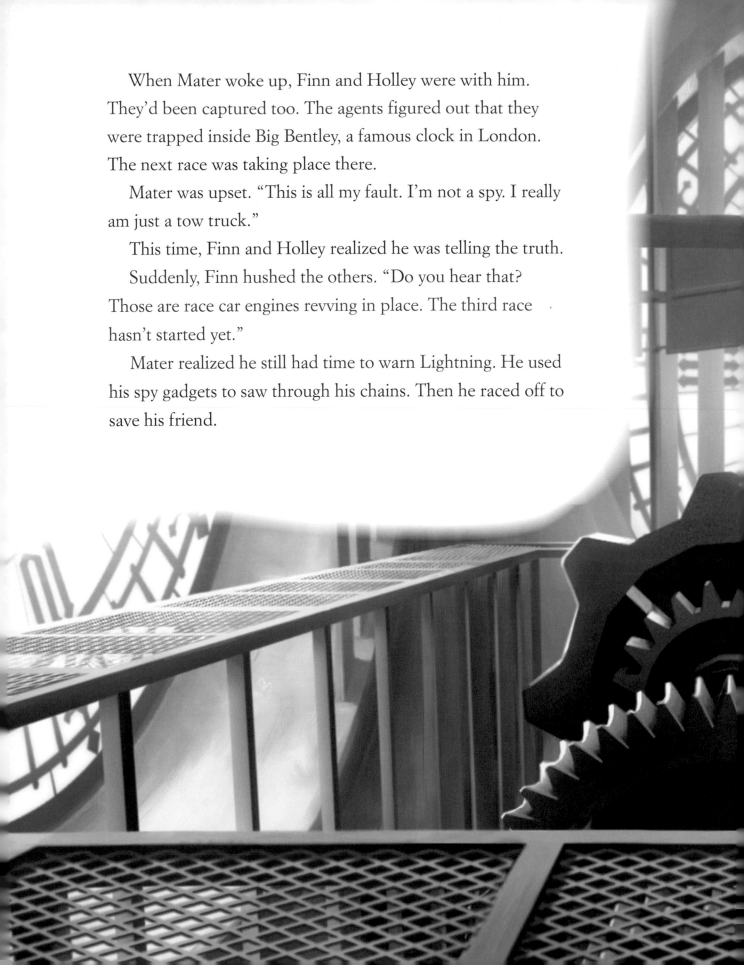

When Mater woke up, Finn and Holley were with him. They'd been captured too. The agents figured out that they were trapped inside Big Bentley, a famous clock in London. The next race was taking place there.

Mater was upset. "This is all my fault. I'm not a spy. I really am just a tow truck."

This time, Finn and Holley realized he was telling the truth.

Suddenly, Finn hushed the others. "Do you hear that? Those are race car engines revving in place. The third race hasn't started yet."

Mater realized he still had time to warn Lightning. He used his spy gadgets to saw through his chains. Then he raced off to save his friend.

When Mater was gone, Holley used her electro-shockers to escape. Finn escaped out the front doors, while Holley smashed through the clock face. The two cars hurried after Mater. They had discovered something terrible. The bad cars had planted a bomb under Mater's hood!

Mater arrived at Lightning's pit. Just then, Finn radioed
him. "The bomb is on you! When we were knocked out, they
planted it in your air filter!"

Mater realized that Finn was right! He zoomed off. He had
to get that bomb as far away from his friend as possible.

When Lightning saw Mater drive onto the racetrack, he forgot
all about the race. His friends from Radiator Springs had told him
Mater had never made it home after the first race. "Mater! I've
been so worried about you."

Mater knew he had to get away from Lightning, so he took off.
"Stay away from me!"

But Lightning followed. "Mater, wait!"

As Lightning chased Mater, Holley followed to try to help.
Finn tried to capture Professor Z.

Soon they all ended up in the same place along with some
of the other bad cars.

Finn had spoken to Professor Z. "Turn off the bomb."

Professor Z rolled his eyes. "Are you all so dense? It's *voice activated*."

Mater couldn't get the words out fast enough: "Deactivate!"

The professor laughed wickedly. "Did I forget to mention that it can only be disarmed by the one who activated it? I'm not the one who activated it."

Suddenly, Mater realized who was responsible. He quickly came up with a plan. He hooked Lightning to him and sped away.

Using his special rocket thrusters, Mater towed Lightning into the air and over London. During the journey he explained to Lightning about the sabotage of the race cars. Mater knew what to do. But they had to move – fast!

The pair landed at the palace, right in front of the Queen of England. Finn and Holley were there too.

Mater turned and saw Sir Axlerod. "It's him. It was you leaking oil at the party. You just blamed it on me."

Holley was confused. "Sir Axlerod created the race, Mater. Why would he want to hurt anyone?"

Mater had realized the engine he'd seen the picture of on the spy plane had been an oil engine that Axlerod used. Axlerod had lied about being an electric car. He was still an oil tycoon – except no one knew. Mater figured out that Axlerod wanted to make Allinol look bad, even though he invented it. Mater knew that if that happened, everyone would want to buy oil and Axlerod would be rich.

At first, no one believed Mater. Then, as the countdown on the bomb went from three seconds to two seconds, Axlerod finally yelled out. "Deactivate!"

The bomb stopped. Axlerod was behind the evil plot, Mater had saved the day!

The Queen was so pleased that she summoned Mater to make him
a knight.

The Lord Steward announced his arrival. "Your Majesty, may I
present for the investiture of honorary knighthood of the British realm,
Tow Mater of Radiator Springs."

Mater rolled forward and bowed.

The Queen smiled and dubbed him a knight.

Mater looked up. He didn't want any fancy titles. "You can just call
me Mater, Your Majesty. I don't want to hear none of this 'Sir' business."

After all the excitement, Mater and Lightning were happy to finally be back home again. Best of all, Lightning decided to hold the Radiator Springs Grand Prix. A temporary racecourse was set up, weaving in and out of the town and nearby area.

Francesco cruised the main street alongside Lightning. The Italian race car thought the final race was a great idea.

Lightning agreed. "Yeah, I just figured, we never found out who the world's fastest car is. Plus: no press, no trophy. Just racing – the way I like it."

Of course, Francesco was still convinced he was going to win. "See you at the finish line!"

Finally, all the race cars made their way to the starting grid. The traffic light in the centre of town changed from red to yellow to green and the race began! The racers sped off, tearing up Main Street.

Lightning and Francesco led the other cars around the wide, sweeping turn of Willy's Butte.

Tourists and the Radiator Springs gang watched from above, honking and cheering Lightning on.

Finn and Holley were there too.

Finn asked Mater to join them on a new mission. "Her Majesty asked for you personally, Mater."

Mater looked at them. "But I told y'all before, I'm not a spy."

Finn smiled. "Spy or not, you're still the smartest, most honest chap we've ever met."

But Mater didn't want to leave his friends. "Thanks, but as much fun as it was hangin' with y'all, this is where I belong."

Still, there was one last thing he wanted to do.

Mater sped down the racetrack, rockets blasting. He passed all the race cars until he was side-by-side with his best friend, Lightning. "Check it out. They let me keep the rockets! *Weee- hee!*"